Editor's Note

The three stories in this book,
   Aladdin and the Wonderful Lamp,
   Saint George and the Dragon,
   and East of the Sun and West of the Moon,
each contain elements of magic and adventure.

   Though most people think Aladdin and the Wonderful Lamp *was part of the original* Arabian Nights, *it was only added when Antoine Galland did his French translation between 1704 and 1717. Scholars do not know whether he wrote the story himself or based it on another folkloric source. It first appeared in English in 1721–1722, and as a children's book in 1805. The version here is adapted from* The Blue Fairy Book *(1891), edited by Andrew Lang.*

   Saint George and the Dragon *is an adaptation of one adventure from the first book of* The Faerie Queene, *written by the English poet Edmund Spenser and first published in 1590.*

   In the middle 1800's Peter Christen Absjørnsen and Jørgen Moe published a collection of Norwegian folktales. The version of East of the Sun and West of the Moon *in this book was adapted from the 1888 edition of George Webbe Dasent's translation of 59 of the stories from that collection.*

Library of Congress Cataloging-in-Publication Data

Aladdin and the wonderful lamp and other tales of adventure.

(A Golden junior classic)
Contents: Aladdin and the wonderful lamp—Saint George and the dragon—East of the sun and west of the moon.
1. Fairy tales. [1. Fairy tales. 2. Folklore]
I. Accardo, Anthony, ill. II. Aladdin. 1987.
III. Saint George and the dragon. 1987. IV. East of the sun and west of the moon. 1987. V. Series.
PZ8.A343 1987   398.2′1 [E]   86-28175
ISBN: 0-307-12808-3
ISBN: 0-307-62808-6 (lib. bdg.)

ALADDIN AND THE WONDERFUL LAMP
and Other Tales of Adventure

Illustrated by Anthony Accardo

Illustrations painted by Kim Ellis

A GOLDEN BOOK · NEW YORK
Western Publishing Company, Inc., Racine, Wisconsin 53404

Copyright © 1987 by Western Publishing Company, Inc. Illustrations copyright © 1987 by Anthony Accardo. All rights reserved. Printed in the U.S.A. No part of this book may be reproduced or copied in any form without written permission from the publisher. GOLDEN®, GOLDEN & DESIGN®, A GOLDEN BOOK®, A GOLDEN CLASSIC®, A GOLDEN JUNIOR CLASSIC®, and A GOLDEN JUNIOR CLASSIC & DESIGN® are trademarks of Western Publishing Company, Inc. CIP data may be found on preceding page. A B C D E F G H I J

Aladdin and the Wonderful Lamp

LONG AGO and far away there lived a poor woman and her son, Aladdin. One day when he was playing in the streets, a stranger asked him, "Aren't you the son of Mustapha the tailor?"

"I am, sir," said Aladdin, "but he died many years ago."

At this the stranger hugged him and said, "Why, I am your uncle! I knew you must be Mustapha's son because you look just like he did at your age. Come, take me to your mother."

When they arrived, Aladdin's mother said, "Mustapha told me he had a brother, but he thought you were dead."

"That is because I went away so long ago," said the uncle. "But now I have returned, and I am only sorry it is too late to see my brother. Tell me about him." So the three talked far into the night.

The next day the uncle took Aladdin for a walk outside the city gates. On and on they walked until they came to the mountains. "We will stop here for a while," said the uncle. "Gather sticks, and I will kindle a fire."

When the fire was lit, the uncle threw some powder on it and uttered a few strange words. The ground trembled and split open, revealing stone steps leading into a deep cavern.

Aladdin was frightened, but the uncle said, "Fear nothing. Do as I say, and you will be rewarded. At the foot of the steps are three halls filled with gold and silver. Go through them, but don't touch anything or you will die instantly. At the end of the last hall there is a garden planted with fruit trees. Walk on until you come to a terrace, where you will find a lamp. Bring it to me."

Aladdin hesitated, still fearful, and the uncle took a ring from his finger and gave it to Aladdin, saying it would keep him safe.

Aladdin found everything as the uncle had said. After he got the lamp, he gathered some fruit and ran back. From the top of the steps the uncle called, "Toss the lamp to me!"

"But you might drop it," said Aladdin.

"I won't," said the uncle. "Now toss it to me!"

"No," said Aladdin. "I'll bring it to you."

"*Toss it!*" shouted the uncle.

When Aladdin still refused, the uncle flew into a rage, threw powder on the fire, and uttered more strange words. With a rumble, the earth closed up, and the uncle hurried off.

Wondering all the while why his uncle had done such a thing, Aladdin tried to find a way out of the cavern. At last he gave up and began to moan and wring his hands. In doing so, he rubbed the ring the uncle had given him. With a loud noise, an enormous genie appeared and said, "I am the genie of the ring and will do anything you wish!"

"I wish I were out of this place!" Aladdin said.

Before he could blink, he found himself outside. Aladdin made his way home as fast as he could, and his mother was overjoyed to see him safe. He told her all that had passed and showed her the lamp and the fruit he had picked.

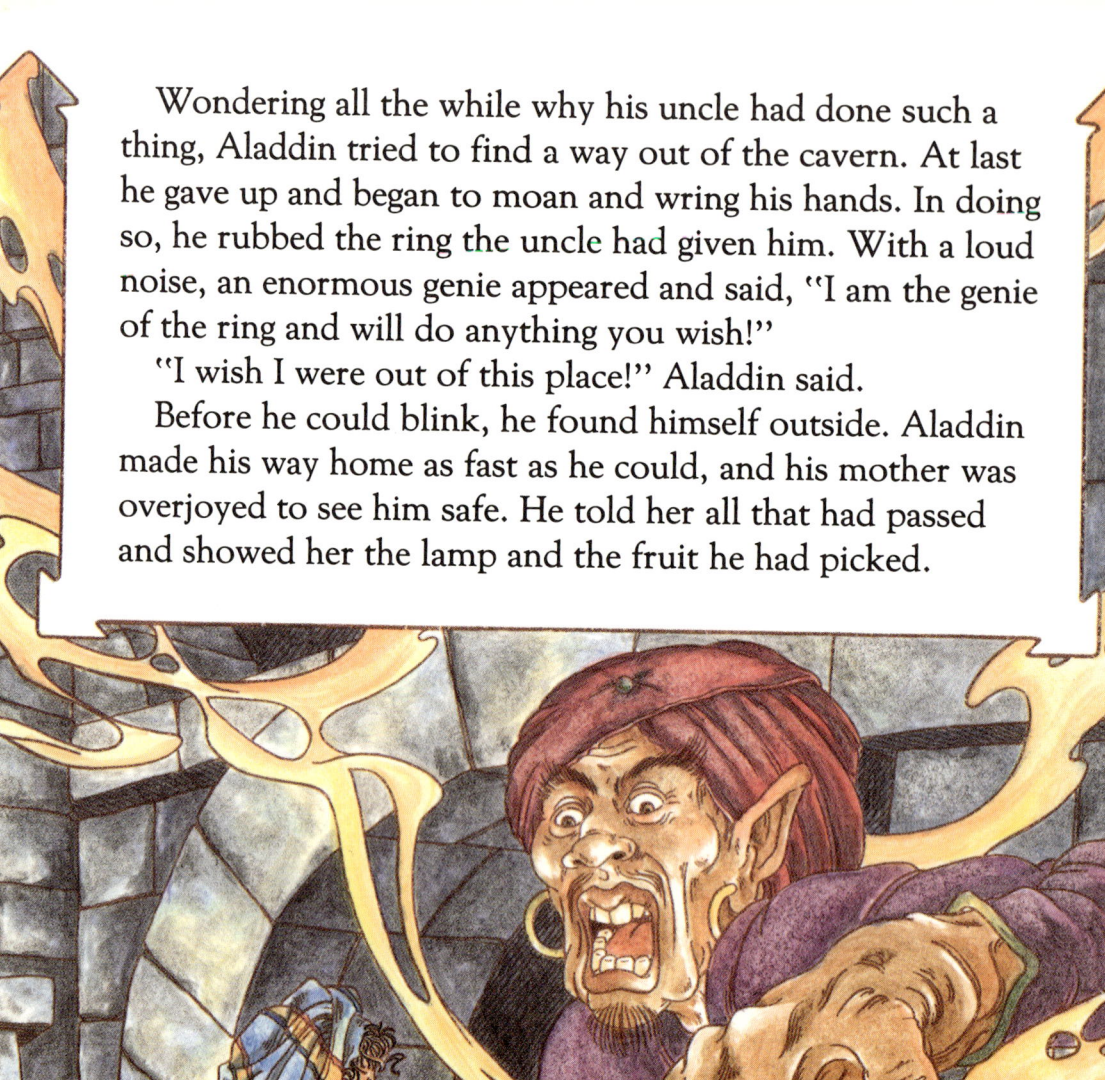

"Why, these are jewels, not fruit!" she said.

"I know," said Aladdin. "That's why I'm starving!"

"Alas, my son, we have neither food nor money."

"Then I will sell the lamp," said Aladdin.

His mother took the lamp to polish it. No sooner had she touched her cloth to it than there was a noise like thunder, and another genie even bigger than the first one appeared. "I am the genie of the lamp," he roared, "and I am at your command!"

Aladdin took the lamp and said, "Bring us something to eat!"

And there before them were twelve silver plates filled with food. After they had eaten, Aladdin sold the plates one by one, and thus he and his mother were able to live for a long time.

One day the sultan proclaimed that everyone was to stay home and close the shutters while the princess rode through the city. Curious, Aladdin peered through the shutters as the princess went by. She lifted her veil, and when Aladdin saw her face, he fell in love with her at once.

He bade his mother go before the sultan on his behalf and ask for the princess's hand in marriage. Aladdin's mother saw that he was serious, and she agreed to go. She took the jeweled fruit from the garden with her to the palace as a gift for the sultan.

When Aladdin's mother knelt before the throne, the sultan said, "Rise, good woman, and tell me what you want."

She hesitated, but the sultan told her to speak up, promising to forgive her for anything she might say. She told him Aladdin's request and ended by saying, "I beg you to accept this gift and forgive not only me, but Aladdin."

When the sultan saw the jeweled fruit, he thought, "Ought I not give the princess to one who values her so highly?" Out loud he said, "Good woman, I will consent to the marriage. Return and tell your son that I await him with open arms."

She lost no time in telling Aladdin, who summoned the genie. "Dress me in fine clothes and bring me a horse better than the sultan's, twenty servants to attend me, and ten thousand pieces of gold."

It was no sooner said than done. Aladdin mounted his horse and rode through the streets, his servants throwing pieces of gold to the people as they went. The sultan met Aladdin at the palace gate, wishing to marry him to the princess at once. But Aladdin said, "First I must build the princess a palace."

Once home, he summoned the genie and told him, "Build me a palace of the finest marble. In the middle I want a great hall with a dome, walls of silver and gold, and windows set with diamonds and rubies. There must be stables, grooms, and servants. Go and see about it."

The palace was ready the next day. That same night Aladdin and the princess were married. For many years they lived in contentment. Aladdin won the hearts of the people with his generosity and gentle ways. The sultan awarded him many responsibilities, and Aladdin's name became known far and wide.

A magician in Africa heard of the poor tailor's son who was now married to the sultan's daughter. This magician was the man who had once pretended to be Aladdin's uncle.

Many years before, he had read of a lamp that contained great power, but the book said it could only be received from the hand of another. The magician had picked the foolish Aladdin to help him, but Aladdin had so angered him, he had closed him up in the cavern without getting the lamp.

The magician was furious to think that Aladdin had escaped and learned the power of the lamp. He set out and traveled day and night until he reached the city. As soon as he saw the magnificent palace built by the genie, he went half mad with rage.

When he learned that Aladdin was away from home, the magician bought a dozen lamps and put them into a basket. He went to the palace, crying, "New lamps for old!"

The princess was sitting in the great hall. When she heard the noise, she sent a servant to see what it was about. The servant came back laughing. "Madam, it is only an old fool offering to exchange fine new lamps for old ones."

"There is an old lamp in the corner," said the princess, not knowing of its power. "Exchange it for a new one."

The servant carried the old lamp outside. The magician knew it at once and snatched it from her hands. As soon as she had chosen a new lamp and returned to the palace, the magician hurried out of the city.

That night the magician commanded the genie to carry him, Aladdin's palace, and everyone in it to Africa.

The next morning the sultan looked out his window and stared in disbelief. Aladdin's palace had disappeared! He sent thirty men on horseback to find him. They met Aladdin riding home and brought him back in chains.

"My dear father-in-law," Aladdin asked, "what have I done?"

"Look!" said the sultan, pointing to the empty space where Aladdin's palace had stood. "Bring back my daughter or I will cut off your head!"

"Allow me forty days to find her," said Aladdin. "If I do not, I will return and suffer death at your pleasure."

The sultan agreed, and Aladdin left the palace. He wandered around in a daze, asking everyone what had become of the palace, but nobody could help him. One night he clasped his hands and, without knowing it, rubbed the magic ring he still wore. There was a loud noise, and the genie of the ring appeared. "What is your will?" he asked.

"Bring my palace back," said Aladdin.

"That I cannot do," replied the genie. "It is not in my power to undo what the genie of the lamp has done."

"Then take me to my palace, wherever it may be," said Aladdin.

He at once found himself at the bedside of the princess. He woke her gently and said, "I beg of you, Princess, tell me what became of the old lamp I left in the great hall."

"Alas!" she cried. "I am the cause of our sorrows!" She told him about the magician who had tricked her. When she described him, Aladdin realized the magician was the uncle.

"So he is not my real uncle at all!" cried Aladdin. "Where is the lamp now?"

"He carries it with him," said the princess. "Every day he visits me and asks me to break my vows to you and marry him, but I only reply with my tears."

"Do not worry," Aladdin said. "All will be well."

Aladdin left the princess and went into the town, where he bought a certain powder in a dark, dusty shop. He then returned to her and said, "Put on your most beautiful dress and invite the magician to dine with you. Say you wish to taste the tea of Africa. He will go to find some, and while he is gone this is what you should do."

The princess listened carefully to Aladdin, and when he left her, she put on her finest clothes. When the magician arrived, she said, "I have made up my mind that Aladdin is dead. All my tears will not bring him back, so I am resolved to mourn no more. You may dine with me if you will bring me the tea of Africa that I might taste it."

The magician hurried to get some. When the magician returned, the princess put the powder Aladdin had given her into his cup. After she poured the tea, the princess said, "Let us drink."

She put her cup to her lips and held it there while the magician drained his to the dregs. His eyes grew wide, and he fell back lifeless. The princess let Aladdin in, and he went to the dead magician, took the lamp from his robe, and summoned the genie.

"Return my palace and all who are in it to its original place," Aladdin commanded.

    The sultan, who was sitting near his window, happened to look up. There stood Aladdin's palace as before! He hastened there, and Aladdin received him in the great hall, with the princess at his side. Aladdin told him what had happened and showed him the body of the magician that he might believe. The sultan proclaimed a great feast, and there was much rejoicing in the city.

    After that, the princess and Aladdin lived in peace. When the sultan died, Aladdin succeeded him and reigned for many years.

Saint George and the Dragon

IN THE DISTANCE rode a knight whose breastplate and shield bore a red cross. Beside him rode a veiled princess on a white donkey. Her name was Una. The princess and the knight were traveling to her kingdom, where a fierce dragon held her people captive. Una had escaped and wandered far in search of a knight who would fight the dragon. After a long time, she had found the Red Cross Knight.

As they rode over the last hill the dragon lay stretched out before them. When it saw them coming, it rose up and gave a terrifying roar. The knight told Una to go where she would be safe while he did battle with the dragon.

As the dreadful beast drew near it shook itself, and the clash of its brass scales was deafening. It opened its wings, which were like two sails of a ship, and lashed its long tail. At the end were two pointed stingers that were as razor sharp as its claws. Iron teeth lined its mouth, and when it roared, fire and smoke billowed forth. The dragon glared at the knight with blazing eyes, and he rushed it, his spear held before him.

The spear found its mark, but slid off the metal scales. The dragon turned and knocked the knight off his horse with its tail. The knight remounted and attacked. Again the spear glanced off, but it gave the dragon a fearful jolt.

Enraged, the beast spread its wings, snatched up the knight and his horse, and carried them through the air. But horse and rider struggled so mightily, the dragon could not stay up. When it landed, the knight struck its neck as hard as he could. The spear slid under the dragon's wing and left a great gash. The dragon roared. Fire poured out of its mouth, singeing the knight's face and making his armor hot as an oven.

The knight fell backward into a spring of water. The dragon thought the battle was over and retreated to rest itself. Now, it happened that the water in which the knight lay was used to heal the sick before the dragon came. As Una watched and prayed the night through, the water healed the knight's wounds.

The next day he rose up again and joined the dragon in battle. It seemed the spring had given him new strength, for he smote the dragon on the head with his sword and left a fearsome wound.

The dragon screamed and lashed its tail. Its stinger went through the knight's shield and pierced his shoulder. With a mighty blow the knight cut the dragon's tail off. In pain and anger, the dragon flew up and grasped the knight's shield with its great claws. Though he struck and struck again, the knight could not free himself. At last his sword slipped between the dragon's scales and cut through one of its feet.

The dragon roared, and flames scorched the knight. He stumbled and fell among the roots of an apple tree, where he lay still. The dragon could not follow him, for it was the tree of life, and the dragon stood for death. That evening a soothing balm trickled down on the knight. As Una watched and prayed the night through, the balm healed the knight's wounds.

The next day he rose up again to fight the sorely wounded dragon. The dragon opened its jaws wide to swallow him, but the knight moved quickly and ran his sword through the dragon's mouth. Down it fell and breathed out all its life.

As the brave knight stood over the fallen dragon, Una and her people gathered around to thank him. Many years and many adventures later this same knight would come to be known as Saint George of England.

East of the Sun and West of the Moon

ONE EVENING, as a storm raged outside, a poor man and his wife sat around the fire with their children, doing this and that. Just as the wind blew its hardest they heard a tapping at the window. When the father went out to see what it was, there stood a great white bear.

"Give me your youngest daughter," said the bear, "and I will make you as rich as you are now poor."

Well, the father did not think he would mind being rich, but he thought he should talk it over with his daughter first. He told the white bear to come back in a week for his answer.

At first his daughter said no, but all that week the father talked about how well off they would be, and at last she agreed. When the white bear returned, she got up on his back and away they went.

After a while, the white bear said, "Are you afraid?"

"Not at all," the girl replied.

On they rode until they came to a high mountain. There the white bear knocked on a great stone, and a door opened. Inside were the rooms of a castle. The white bear gave the girl a silver bell and told her to ring it whenever she wanted anything.

After supper, the girl felt sleepy and thought she would like to go to bed. She rang the bell and instantly found herself in a beautiful bedroom. No sooner had she put out the light and gone to bed than a man came in and lay down beside her. Before morning he was gone.

So things went for a while, but at last the girl grew sad. One day the white bear asked her what was the matter. "I miss my family," she replied.

"I will take you to see them," said the bear, "but you must promise not to speak alone with your mother. If you do, you'll bring bad luck on both of us."

The next day the white bear took the girl on his back, and on they rode until they came to a grand house. "Here you are," he said. "Don't forget your promise."

When the girl greeted her family, there was such joy, there was no end to it. That afternoon, when her mother tried to draw her away, the girl said, "Oh, we can talk later." But somehow or other, her mother got her alone, and the girl told her everything. "If only I could see him just once," she ended her story.

"Take this candle," said her mother. "Light it when the man is asleep, but be careful not to drop any tallow on him."

In the evening the white bear came to take the girl home.

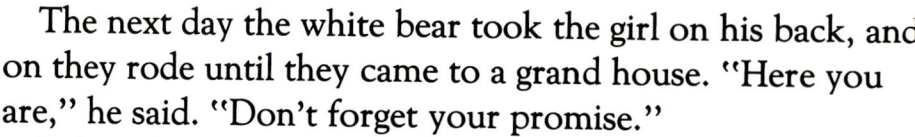

That night, when the girl lit the candle, she saw the most handsome man she had ever set eyes on. But as she leaned over him three drops of hot tallow fell on his shirt and woke him up.

"Look what you've done!" he cried. "A troll woman bewitched me so that I am a white bear by day and a man by night. If only you had waited one year, I would have been free. Now I must go to the castle that lay east of the sun and west of the moon and marry her daughter with the long nose."

"Can I go with you?" the girl asked.

"No," he replied.

"Then I'll search for you," she said.

Next morning the girl rubbed the sleep from her eyes and set out. After many days, she came to a high crag. There sat an old hag, tossing a golden apple from hand to hand.

"Do you know the way to the castle that lay east of the sun and west of the moon?" the girl asked.

"Are you the one who should have married the prince who's shut up there?" said the old hag.

"I am," said the girl.

"All I know," said the old hag, "is that thither you'll come, late or never. Still, you may borrow my horse and ride to my next neighbor. Maybe she'll be able to tell you the way. Here, take this golden apple with you."

The girl rode until she came to another crag under which sat a second old hag. "Do you know the way to the castle that lay east of the sun and west of the moon?" the girl asked.

"I know nothing about it, but thither you'll come, late or never, and you may borrow my horse to ride to my next neighbor. Maybe she'll know the way." And this old hag gave the girl a golden carding-comb.

The girl rode until she came to another great crag where sat a third old hag. "Do you know the way to the castle that lay east of the sun and west of the moon?" she asked.

"No," said the old hag, "but thither you'll come, late or never, and I'll lend you my horse to ride to the East Wind. Maybe he can help you." She gave the girl a golden spinning wheel to take with her.

The girl rode many days. When she got to the East Wind's house, she asked, "Do you know the way to the castle that lay east of the sun and west of the moon?"

"No," said the East Wind. "But if you're not afraid, I will take you to my brother the West Wind. Maybe he knows."

When they got there, the West Wind told the girl he had never blown so far. "But if you're not afraid, I will take you to our brother the South Wind. He is stronger than either of us. Perhaps he can help you."

But the South Wind said, "I have never been so far as the castle that lay east of the sun and west of the moon. Still, if you're not afraid, I'll take you to our strongest brother, the North Wind. If he can't help you, nobody can."

"What do you want?" roared the North Wind when they got to his house.

"You needn't be cross," said the South Wind. "Here is the one who should have married the prince who lives in the castle east of the sun and west of the moon. Can you tell her the way?"

"Once I blew there," said the North Wind, "but I was so tired, I couldn't even puff for days. If you aren't afraid," he said to the girl, "I'll see if I can blow you there."

"I'm not afraid," she answered.

"Very well," said the North Wind. "But we must wait until morning, for we will need the whole day if we are to get there at all."

Early the next day the North Wind puffed himself up and blew off, taking the girl with him. On and on they rushed, all the time over the sea. The North Wind got wearier and wearier. At last he could hardly puff. He sank so low, the waves washed over the girl's ankles.

"Are you afraid?" he asked her.

"Not at all," she replied.

At last they saw land. The North Wind had just enough breath left to blow the girl up on the shore near the castle that lay east of the sun and west of the moon.

Next morning the girl sat under the castle windows, playing with the golden apple. A troll with a long nose leaned out a window and asked, "What do you want for your golden apple?"

"Let me stay the night with the prince who lives here," said the girl, "and you can have it."

"Done," said the troll.

That night, when the girl got to the prince's bedroom, he was fast asleep. She called him and shook him, but nothing would wake him up. In the morning the troll chased the girl out.

Later on she sat under the castle windows and began to card with her golden carding-comb. The troll wanted it, and the girl said if she could stay the night with the prince, the troll could have it.

That night the girl again found the prince sound asleep, and nothing she could do would rouse him. The next morning she had to leave.

In the afternoon the girl sat under the castle windows and began to spin with her golden spinning wheel. That, too, the troll wanted. The girl told her she would only part with it if she could stay the night with the prince. "So you may," said the troll.

Now, it happened that there were some poor folk shut up in the room next to the prince. That day they told him about the woman they had heard weeping and calling to him at night. When the troll brought his evening chocolate, the prince only pretended to drink it, for he guessed she had put a sleeping potion in it. That night the girl found the prince wide awake.

"You are just in time," he said. "Tomorrow I am to marry the troll with the long nose, and you are the only one who can save me. Before the wedding, I'll refuse to marry anyone but the woman who can wash the tallow out of my shirt. Stay close to the castle, because the troll won't be able to do it. When she fails, I'll call you."

The next day the prince said, "I have sworn never to take a bride unless she can wash this tallow out of my shirt. If she can't do that, she's not worth marrying."

"Ha!" said the troll. "That's easy." She began to scrub the shirt, but the harder she scrubbed, the bigger the spots grew.

"Let me try," said her mother. But with all her rubbing and scrubbing, the spots just grew bigger and blacker.

Then all the other trolls tried, but the harder they rubbed, blacker the shirt grew.

"None of you are worth a straw," said the prince. "Why, I'll bet that beggar girl sitting outside can wash better than any of you. Come here," he called to the girl. "Can you wash this shirt clean?"

"I don't know," she said, "but I think I can." And almost before she had dipped it in the water, the shirt was as white as the driven snow, and whiter still.

"Well, you're the one for me," said the prince.

At that the troll mother flew into such a rage, she burst on the spot, and her daughter after her, and the whole pack of trolls after her.

Then the North Wind, who was rested up by that time, blew the girl and the prince all the way home, where they were married.